Enid Blyton's

MAGICAL TALES

The Adventurous Duck

and other stories

This is a Parragon Book

© Parragon 1997

13-17 Avonbridge Trading Estate,
Atlantic Road, Avonmouth, Bristol
Produced by The Templar Company plc,
Pippbrook Mill, London Road, Dorking,
Surrey RH4 1JE

Text copyright © Enid Blyton Ltd 1926-29

These stories were first published in Sunny Stories,
Teacher's Treasury, Two Years in the Infant School,
Read to Us, New Friends and Old and
The Daily Mail Annual.

Enid Blyton's signature mark is a registered
trademark of Enid Blyton Limited.

Edited by Caroline Repchuk and Dugald Steer

Designed by Mark Kingsley-Monks

Printed and bound in Italy

ISBN 0 7525 1708 2 (Hardback)
ISBN 0 7525 2321 X (Paperback)

Enid Blyton's

The Adventurous Duck

and other stories

PARRAGON

Contents

The Adventurous Duck

TIMOTHY had some money that his uncle had given him to spend. So he went to the toy shop on the seafront to buy something with it. He chose a very fine, floating duck, and ran with it down to the sea.

It floated beautifully. It bobbed up and down on the waves, and looked lovely. All the other boys and girls watched it and thought Timothy was very lucky.

But the duck was too adventurous. It floated out too far, and Timothy couldn't get it back again. On it went and on and on, right out to sea. Timothy watched it go sadly, for it really was a very beautiful duck.

Soon the duck was frightened. It couldn't see Timothy any more, and the sea was very large and very deep. Fishes swam about beneath it, and great seagulls sailed in the sky overhead.

"I wish I hadn't been so adventurous," said the duck, sadly. "I wish I had kept close to Timothy. Now I shall be lost and never see him again."

Suddenly the duck gave a frightened quack, and trembled all down its plastic body. A big seagull was swooping nearer and nearer. At last it pounced on the little floating duck, and picked it up in its yellow beak. Then away up in the air it flew, carrying the duck with it.

Higher and higher it went, and the other gulls came flying round to see what their friend held in his beak.

"Silly! Silly!" they cried. "It's nothing you can eat! It's just a stupid toy!"

The gull gave a screech, and dropped the duck again.

Far below, the duck saw a boat full of people. A little girl was sitting in the boat, and she suddenly saw the falling duck. She held out her hands, and caught it just like a ball.

"Why, it's a dear little floating duck!" she cried out in astonishment. "Oh, I really *must* take it out to tea with me this afternoon!"

So when she was rowed to the shore, and trotted off to go to tea with her Auntie, she took the little duck with her. Her cousin was waiting for her at the gate and she waved to him.

"Come and look at what I've got!" she cried. "It's a dear little floating duck that fell out of a gull's beak!"

Now, who do you suppose her cousin was? Why, it was

Timothy! He stared at the duck
in surprise, for he could see that
it was his.

"Why, that's the little duck I
bought with the money your
Daddy gave me this morning!"
he said. "It floated right away
out to sea, and I saw a gull swoop
down and pick it up!"

"And it dropped it into my
hands!" cried the little girl. "Oh,
what an adventure it has had,
Timothy! Here it is, and I hope it
will be a good duck now, and not
go off by itself any more!"

Timothy took it in delight. He
thought he had lost his floating
duck for ever. He was pleased,

and the little girl was pleased, and as for the floating duck, it was so full of joy that it couldn't even quack!

A Knot in his Tail

THE clockwork mouse was always very busy. He ran here and there, he sniffed under the mats and he poked his sharp little nose down every hole he could find.

Sometimes he hid a crumb under the end of the hearthrug.

"Now that fat old teddy bear won't find it!" he said to himself. "I'll remember to come and get it tomorrow."

But he had such a bad memory that he never remembered where he put anything. Teddy would often find the crumb before he did, and that really did make Mouse most awfully cross.

"I wish I could remember better," he said to his friend, the little black doll. "I do really. How can I remember things, Lotty?"

"Well," said Lotty, "when I want to remember something I always tie a little knot in a corner of my hanky – like this, – and then when I see the knot, I say to myself, 'Ah, I put that knot there to remind me to do this or that.' And that's how I always remember."

"That's a very good idea," said the clockwork mouse. "It really is. I'll do it myself.

Oh, bother! I can't!"

"Why can't you?" asked the black doll.

"Because I haven't got a hanky," said Mouse. "You can't tie knots in a hanky if you haven't got one."

"I'll lend you one and you can keep it in your pocket," said Lotty.

"No, I can't," said Mouse. "I haven't got a pocket. I've often felt all over me for one, but I know I haven't got one."

"Well, then, I really don't know *what* you can do!" said Lotty. "Oh, wait a minute – yes, I do !"

"What can I do?" said Mouse, excited.

"You can tie a knot in your tail!" said the little black doll. "Then, when you see the knot, it will remind you that you must remember something."

"That's a very good idea!" said Mouse. "I want to remember where I put a tiny bit of chocolate, Lotty. I put it down the hole that is by the fireplace. I'm going to eat it when I feel hungry."

"Well, tie a knot in your tail, then, and you will remember about the chocolate whenever you see the knot," said Lotty.

So the clockwork mouse tied a beautiful knot in his long tail. Then, before he and Lotty could talk any more, Jane, the little girl whose toys they were, came into the playroom and picked Lotty up.

"You're coming for a ride in my toy pram," she said. "I'm taking you to play next door. Come along, Lotty!"

Now, it was a funny thing, but Mouse didn't notice the knot in his tail at all. He really wasn't used to looking at his tail. He took no notice of it, unless somebody happened to tread on it, then he squealed. So he didn't see the knot again, and he forgot all about it. Lotty had been lent to the little girl next door, and didn't come back – so she couldn't remind him about it, either.

It was Teddy who told him about it. "Mouse!" he cried, "Somebody has played a trick on you!"

"Whatever do you mean?" asked Mouse.

"Well, look at your tail!" said Teddy "Someone has crept up behind you, when you were asleep, and tied your tail into a knot! Ho ho ho!"

The mouse looked at his tail.

He felt very cross indeed to think that anyone should dare to creep up behind him and do such a thing. He glared round at the toys.

"Who's done this unkind thing? I shall bite the one who did it! My tail hurts dreadfully with a knot in it!"

That wasn't true. It didn't hurt a bit. But Mouse loved to make a fuss. He tried to undo the knot, but he couldn't. It was really tied very tight indeed.

"Oh, it's too bad!" he wept. "I can't undo it! It's hurting me. Whatever shall I do, whatever shall I do?"

"*I'll* undo it," said Teddy, with a giggle. But he was very rough with his big paws, and the mouse squealed so loudly that Angela, the biggest doll, made the bear stop trying to undo the knot.

Mouse made quite a puddle on the floor with his tears. Angela felt sorry for him.

"It's a shame, Mouse," she said. "It really is. People oughtn't to tie knots in someone else's tail. Whoever did it ought to be punished."

"Can I bite the horrid person hard?" asked Mouse, a large

tear dripping off the end of his whiskers.

"That would not be a nice thing to do, Mouse," said Angela. "Let's find out who it was and we'll punish them fairly. Somebody here must have done it. Now, I think we are all truthful toys. I'll ask everyone, and whoever did it, even if it was for a joke, must own up. I'm sure no one is too cowardly to own up."

"I'm certain that horrid Teddy did it," wept Mouse.

"I didn't do it, so there!" said Teddy crossly. "I might have, if I'd thought of it – but I just

didn't think of it – and if I had
I'd have put at least twelve
knots into your silly tail, not
one! Ho ho ho!"

"You're horrid," said Mouse.
"If you'd got a tail at all, which
you haven't, I'd nibble the end
right off!"

"Don't talk like that," said
Angela, shocked. "It sounds
most unkind. Now, you didn't
do it, Teddy. Was it you Sailor
Doll?"

"No, of course not" said the
sailor doll at once.

"Did you, Yellow Dog?"
asked Angela, turning to the
dirty old yellow dog who had

lived in the playroom almost longer than any of them. He shook his old head.

"No, I didn't," he said. "I'm too old to play tricks like that."

Angela asked every toy in the nursery, and they all said no, they hadn't tied the knot in Mouse's tail. It was very puzzling.

"Somebody's not telling the truth!" said Mouse, fiercely. "And that's even worse than tying a knot in my tail. I think I'm going to bite the person *very* hard when we find out who it is, even if it isn't very nice of me."

"We'll see about that," said Angela. "We can't do anything until we find out who it is. Wait a bit, though – Lotty isn't here. Maybe it's Lotty! We'll ask her when she comes back."

Lotty came back that evening. The toys crowded round her to hear her news. It wasn't often that any of them went away to stay.

Then Angela asked her about the knot in Mouse's tail. "We're all rather worried," she said, "because some cruel toy has tied a knot in the clockwork mouse's tail, and we don't know who. We can't undo the knot, and it hurts poor Mouse terribly. I do hope it isn't you, Lotty, because we always thought you were Mouse's friend."

"So I am," said Lotty, and she laughed suddenly. "No, I didn't tie the knot. But I know who did! Ho ho ho!"

"Ah! You know who did?" cried Mouse, and he looked very fierce. "Tell me, then, and I'll bite him hard!"

"You tied it yourself, Mouse!" said Lotty, and she laughed again. "Ho ho ho! – what a memory you've got!"

"Tied a knot in my own tail!"

cried Mouse, scornfully. "Why should I do such a silly thing?"

"It wasn't such a silly thing," said Lotty. "Don't you remember saying you wished you had a hanky so that you could tie a knot in it to remind you that you had hidden a bit of chocolate down the hole by the fireplace? And I said, 'Well, tie a knot in your tail instead,' – and you did!"

The toys all stared at the clockwork mouse. He went red to the tip of his nose. "Oh," he said. "Yes. I do remember now. Oh, dear me!"

"Ho ho ho!" roared Teddy.

"He did it himself. Mouse, go and bite yourself very, very hard for being so naughty as to put a knot in your own tail. Ho ho ho!"

"You've been rather silly, haven't you?" said Angela, and Mouse ran away and hid in a dark corner. He looked at his tail. He undid the knot quite easily with his teeth. Then he remembered the bit of chocolate that the knot was supposed to remind him about. He ran to the hole where he had hidden it away.

But it had gone! Teddy had been to find it, and had eaten it up. He had a tiny smear of chocolate on his nose. He saw Mouse looking for it and laughed.

"*I* don't need a knot in *my* tail to help my memory!" he said. "I'm not so silly as you are, Mouse!"

The Cross
Old Man

DAN and Daisy were staying at the seaside. It was lovely. The sky was blue, the sun was hot, the sea was as blue as the sky.

The twins paddled in the sea and dug in the sand and bathed all day long. They played with the other children and built some very fine castles with lovely, big moats.

One afternoon, when the children were building a fort out of the sand, Dan looked down the beach towards the sea to find out whether the tide was coming in. They wanted to finish building the fort before the sea came right up and washed it away.

"Oh look – the tide *is* coming in – and it's almost reached right up to the feet of that old man," said Dan. "Do you suppose he knows? Look, the man in the deckchair over there, I mean!"

"Well, he's looking out to sea, so I suppose he can see the tide coming in!" said Janet. "And anyway, he's a horrid old man. He's always cross and shouting."

The tide crept right up to the old man's feet. Dan was surprised that he didn't move.

He ran down and had a good look at him.

"He's asleep!" he said to the others. "I do think we ought to wake him."

"Well, when my dog barked and woke him up on the beach yesterday he was very cross. He shouted at me and then he threw a stone at my poor dog," said Jim.

"That was very horrid of him," said Daisy. "No, don't wake him up, Dan. Let him stay there and get wet."

"No, we can't do that," said Dan. "You know what Mother always says – if people do

horrid things to you, it is no
reason why you should do
horrid things to them. I think I
am going to wake him up –
even if he does shout at me for
doing it!"

So Dan went to wake the old
man. He touched him gently on
the arm.

"Wake up, sir! The tide is
coming in."

The old man woke up.

"Dear me! So it is! What a
very kind little boy you are!
Thank you!"

And do you know what the
old man did? He bought ice-
creams for every one of the

children on the beach who were building the fort! What a lovely surprise that was! He wasn't such a cross old man after all! Dan *was* so glad he had woken him up.

The Magic Needle

TRICKS and Slippy were tailors. They made coats and cloaks for all the little folk in Breezy Village and the other villages round about.

"We don't get paid nearly enough for our work," grumbled Tricks. "We ought to get *ever* so much more!"

"Yes. If we were paid properly, we should have a nice little motor-car by now to deliver all our goods," said Slippy.

"Oh, you and your motor-car. You're always talking about that," said Tricks. "Now what *I* want is a lovely little ship to sail on the river."

"Fiddlesticks!..." began Slippy, and then he had to stop because a customer had just come in. It was Jinky the brownie. He flung a coat down on the table.

"Look there!" he said. "Bad work again! All the buttons fell off in a day, and this collar has come unstitched. No wonder we don't pay you top prices, you're so careless!"

He stalked out, looking very cross. "Blow!" said Slippy, picking up the coat. "Now I've got to sew those horrid little buttons on all over again. I wish we had a magic needle, Tricks. That's what we want. But nowadays nobody ever hears of a thing like that."

"A magic needle!" said Tricks, looking up in excitement. "Why – my old Granny used to have one. She did, she did! I'd forgotten about it all these years, but now I've suddenly remembered it."

"Goodness! A *real* magic needle?" said Slippy, amazed. "Where is it?"

"Well – I suppose my old Granny has still got it somewhere," said Tricks.

"Go and ask her to lend it to us," said Slippy at once.

"Ooooh, no. I wouldn't dare.

She doesn't like me," said Tricks. "She says I'm always up to tricks, and she shouts at me whenever she sees me, so I never go to see her now."

"What a pity," said Slippy. "Shall *I* go and see her? She might show me the needle, mightn't she – and oh, Tricks! I've just thought of a most wonderful *idea*!"

"What?" said Tricks. "I don't really think much of your ideas, you know."

"Listen, I'll go and visit your Granny and I'll get her to show me the needle – then I'll take her needle and put one of our needles in its place! See?"

"Yes! Yes, that's quite a good idea," said Tricks, pleased. "I know the size it was – and it had a very big eye, I remember. I believe I've got one that looks just like it!"

He hunted about in his box of needles, and took one out. "Here it is – just like Granny's magic one – except that there's no magic in *this* one!"

"Does the real magic one sew all by itself?" asked Slippy.

"Oh, yes – it sews and sews and sews. You've only got to place it on top of a pile of cloth, and say 'Coats' or 'Cloaks', and the needle sets to work at once, and hey presto, there's a pile of coats sitting there before you know where you are!"

"Does it cut the cloth up, too, before it sews it?" asked Slippy, astonished.

"Not exactly," said Tricks. "It sews the cloth into the right shapes – sleeves and so on – and then all the bits and pieces fall away, the coat turns itself inside out, and there you are!"

"Marvellous! Wonderful!" said Slippy. "I'd simply love to see that happen."

"Well, you will if you go to see my Granny," grinned Tricks.

"But be very careful of her when you go, because she's very fond of scolding people."

Slippy set off the very next day with Tricks' needle in a needle case. He caught the bus and went to Hush-Hush Village. He soon came to the house of Tricks' grandmother, a lovely, neat little place with pretty curtains in all the windows.

The old lady didn't seem very pleased to see him. "Hm!" she said, "So you're Slippy, a friend of Tricks, are you? Slippy by name and Slippy by nature, I wouldn't be at all surprised. What have *you* come for?"

"Just to see you," said Slippy. "Tricks has said such a lot about you. He said you were *such* a nice old lady, and so very friendly and kind."

"Hm! Did he tell you I've been kind enough to scold him a hundred times for his bad ways and mischievous tricks?" said the old lay. "Tell him to come and see me again, because I've got scolding number one-hundred-and-one waiting for him."

Slippy began to think that Tricks' grandmother wasn't a very kind old lady.

"Er – is it true that you once had a magic needle?" he asked, thinking that he had better find out before some kind of scolding came *his* way.

"Quite true," said the old woman. "Look in the bottom drawer of that chest, in the left-hand corner, and you'll see a pin-cushion. The needle is stuck in it. Bring it out and I'll show you what it can do."

Slippy found the needle easily. He took it out of the pin-cushion excitedly and gave it to the old woman. She threaded it with red cotton, pulled Slippy's lovely new red hanky out of his pocket and stuck the needle into the corner of it.

"Doll's dress," she said, in a loud voice. And, to Slippy's enormous surprise, that needle set to – and, in no time at all, there was a beautiful little doll's dress lying on the table, all frills and bows! The needle had slipped in and out so fast, with a long red thread behind it, that Slippy had found it quite difficult to follow.

"Marvellous!" said Slippy. "But what about my lovely new hanky? You shouldn't have made a doll's dress out of it."

"Don't you talk to me like that," said the old lady, as if she was going to shout at Slippy.

"You'll just have to blow your nose on a doll's dress, that's all. And if you dare to ..."

Slippy fled! He pushed the red doll's dress into his pocket. He was grinning broadly. Aha! He had just had time to exchange the two needles! He had the magic one in his needle-case – and he had left the one he had brought, safely pushed into the pin-cushion!

Tricks was delighted when Slippy showed him the needle. "Well done, Slippy!" he said. "I never thought you'd be able to get it. Granny's eyes are so sharp, I was sure she'd spot you exchanging the needles. *Now* we'll be able to make some money. My word, we'll be able to make some money! My word, we'll be able make a dozen coats a day now!"

"I didn't like your granny," said Slippy. "She was rather rude to me, I thought she was going to start shouting at me."

"She probably was," said Tricks. "Well, we will never, never go near her again, so we won't have any more trouble from her. Now – let's go out and buy all kinds of cloth, and get that needle to start working on new coats tonight."

So out they went and spent a lot of money on new cloth. They staggered home with it, and set it on the table.

"Yellow cloth, red cloth, blue, purple, black, green and scarlet," said Tricks. "My, what a wonderful lot of handsome coats we'll have! Needle, listen to me. Here are reels of cotton to match each cloth. You are a sensible needle, and will take the right cotton from each reel. I will thread you the first time, and after that you will thread yourself, just as you used to do for my Granny!"

"Most remarkable," said

Slippy, watching him in delight.
Tricks threaded the magic needle
with red cotton and then stuck it
into a pile of red cloth.

"Coats!" he said, and dear me,
you should have seen that
needle! It flew in and out, in and
out, and there were the two
sleeves and soon the collar was
made, and the lapels, and the
coat itself, – and then the sleeves
were sewn in, quick as lightning.

"Buttons! We've forgotten the
buttons," said Slippy suddenly,
and he rushed out to buy buttons
of all colours. The needle was
wonderful with buttons. It sewed
them all on in the right places, as

quick as a flash and as strongly as could be!

"There's the *first* coat," said Tricks, pleased. "And look at all the bits and pieces that have fallen off just as if they'd been cut away. Really, this is a very powerful needle."

"It is," said Slippy. "Shall we have our supper and go to bed? I don't really want to watch the needle making coats all night long. It's rather tiring to see something working so hard."

So they had buns and cocoa and went off to bed, leaving the magic needle flying in and out as if it was worked by lightning!

What a very fine thing!

They fell asleep in their two little beds. The needle went on working by itself in the workroom. In three hours it had finished the pile of coats – sixteen beautifully finished coats lay in a heap, with shiny little buttons down the fronts.

The needle had no more cloth. It took a look round with its one eye. Ah – what about the tablecloth? It must make a coat out of that. So it did – and a very nice little check coat it was!

Then it took another look round. Ah – what about that hearth rug? That would make a fine warm coat!

And down swooped the needle and in about ten minutes there was no rug to be seen – but in its place was a very warm little coat, with snippings on the floor around it!

The needle was really enjoying itself tremendously. It made coats out of the curtains. It tried to make one out of a cushion, but it couldn't. It made coats out of the dusters, and teacloths, and even out of a pair of stockings. Really, it was a remarkably ingenious needle.

Soon there was nothing left downstairs for it to sew. So it

flew upstairs, looking round with its one eye. When it saw all the bedclothes on the two beds it was simply delighted!

And very soon it was busy making coats out of all the sheets and blankets on Slippy's bed. But as Slippy was lying fast asleep in them, it made things very difficult for the needle. It had to join all the coats together around Slippy, and in the end the bed looked like an enormous sack with sleeves sticking out of it here, there and everywhere! Slippy couldn't be seen – he was inside somewhere!

He woke up and began to

wriggle. Whatever had happened? Where was he? He called out to Tricks. But Tricks was now being sewn up, too, in half a dozen coats which were made up of *his* sheets and blankets, and even one of the corners of his eiderdown. Oh dear, oh dear!

Slippy and Tricks shouted and wriggled and they both rolled off their beds with a bump. What a dreadful night they had! The needle couldn't quite understand what had happened and kept going up to them and pricking them. That made them yell all the more!

They rolled to the door. They bumped all the way down the little flight of stairs – bumpity-bumpity-bump-*bump*!

But they couldn't undo themselves, because when that needle sewed, it sewed very well indeed!

"Slippy! We'll have to roll out of the door and into the front garden," gasped Tricks at last. "We simply must get help. It's morning now, because I can hear the milkman coming."

He rolled himself hard against the door and it burst open. Out went Slippy and Tricks, looking most peculiar all sewn up in sheets and blankets, with long sleeves flapping about all over the place!

The milkman was amazed. He dropped his milk-can and stood there, staring.

"Help! Help!" he shouted. "There's something very strange going on here!"

Well, very soon the neighbours came out and found out just what had happened. Tricks told them about the antics of the magic needle, and begged his friends to snip the stitches and let him out.

At last he was freed from the mass of sheet-and-blanket coats, and stood up, blinking in the sunlight. And, oh dear – when he saw his curtains and carpet and table cloth and everything else made into coats, he wept loudly. So did Slippy.

"The needle's still busy!" cried Slippy, suddenly. "Look, it's got into our chest of drawers and it's making coats out of our vests and pants and trousers and *everything*!"

"We'll have to take it back to my Granny," said Tricks, tears streaming down his face. "Come on. It's no good, that needle will go on and on till it's taken back. We'll be ruined!"

So they had to take the needle
back. How they hoped the old
lady would be out. But she
wasn't! She was watching for
them. *She* knew that Slippy had
exchanged the needles – her eyes
were as just sharp as the eye of
that needle!

Well, you can guess what
happened, and why Slippy and
Tricks went home howling, and
looked sorry for themselves for a
whole week. Nobody would buy
the coats the needle had made –
they said they were afraid of
magic coats. So it didn't do them
much good to play a silly trick
like that on Tricks' grandmother

– in fact, they are still trying to undo the stitches in the curtain-coats, and rug-coat and tablecloth-coat, to get them back again.

That needle has taught them not to be lazy, anyhow!

Big-Hands
the Goblin

ONCE upon a time Nobbly the gnome quarrelled with Big-Hands the goblin. They lived next door to one another and had always been good friends till this quarrel.

It was a very silly quarrel, really. It just so happened that Tip-tap the butcher had called at Nobbly's with his meat, and Nobbly was out. So the butcher had left it on the window-sill – and when Nobbly came home he saw Big-Hands' cat licking the meat!

He rushed in to Big-Hands' cottage in a furious rage. "That cat of yours has licked my meat!"

he cried. "Smack it, Big-Hands, smack it!"

"Certainly not", said Big-Hands, who was very fond of his cat. "I never smack anything. And how can you expect a cat not to lick meat if it is left out on a window-sill? You should go and tell the butcher off for doing such a foolish thing. Why, any other cat but mine would have stolen the meat and taken it away to eat it! I think my cat should be praised, not punished for only just licking the meat. It must very badly have wanted to steal that meat of yours away altogether!"

Just at that moment the cat came in, licking its lips. Nobbly flew at it, and began chasing it around the room, so that it mewed in dismay and fled into a corner.

Big-Hands was very angry. He rushed at Nobbly and grabbed him – but Nobbly was far too bony a person to hold on to. He had great, bony feet and long, skinny arms and a knobbly head. Big-Hands soon let him go and then Nobbly fled to his cottage, crying "I'll pay you back for this, so I will!"

And he did too. He really was very naughty indeed. He threw

all his rubbish over the wall into Big-Hands' garden. He lit his bonfire when the wind was blowing towards Big-Hands' cottage, so the poor gnome had his kitchen filled with smoke all day long. And he played some very loud music indeed when he knew that Big-Hands was having his afternoon nap!

This made the gnome very angry. He ran up the path to Nobbly's front door and banged on the knocker. Nobbly wouldn't open the door, so Big-Hands stood on the doorstep and yelled at him.

"I'm going to pay you back for

all these unkind things! Yes, you look out, Nobbly! You'll be sorry for yourself, you will! I'll just show you what I can do! Grrrrrr!"

Big-Hands sounded so very fierce that Nobbly really felt rather frightened. Big-Hands did not usually lose his temper, for he was good-natured fellow, but when he did people knew all about it!

Nobbly looked at Big-Hands going down the path, from behind the curtain. He saw him doubling up his big hands into fists, and shaking them, uttering angrily all the time.

"Ooooh!" thought Nobbly. "I'd better be careful. There's really no knowing what Big-Hands might do!"

So that day Nobbly didn't throw any more rubbish over the wall, and he didn't play any more music, either. He went up to bed early that night, read a book for a little while and then fell fast asleep.

When he woke up, the moon was shining brightly outside his window. And, to Nobbly's great fright and horror, he suddenly saw what looked like two enormous hands sticking up at the end of his bed, looking for all the world, as if they belonged to someone crouching behind the foot of the bed, ready to pounce out on him!

Nobbly turned pale and shivered so that the bed shook very much indeed. His hair stood up on end.

"It's Big-Hands the goblin come to scare me!" he groaned to himself. "Oh my, oh my, look at those awful great hands sticking up there, ready to come at me if I so much as speak a single word."

Now, Nobbly had made a very great mistake. What he thought were hands were not hands at all

– but simply his own great bony feet sticking up out of the bed clothes! Nobbly was so bony that the clothes found it difficult to keep on him, and were for ever slipping off!

Nobbly lay and looked at his feet, thinking all the time that they were hands and wondering what in the world he could do to frighten away Big-Hands, whom he was absolutely sure was hiding at the end of the bed. Then suddenly the moon went behind a cloud and the room became pitch dark. Nobbly decided to creep out of bed and light his candle.

He crept out, and went to the table by the wall where his candle stood. He lit it and then held it up to see Big-Hands – but, of course, there was no one at the end of the bed at all! No – there wasn't a sign of Big-Hands the goblin at all! It really was most puzzling!

"He's gone!" said Nobbly, pleased. "Oh, what a fright he gave me, the horrid creature! What shall I do if he comes again tomorrow night? I shouldn't ever dare to go to bed again! It really won't do at all. I must go and complain to Mr Stick, the policeman at once."

So, the next morning Nobbly went to the cottage where Mr Stick the policeman lived. He was just finishing his morning cup of cocoa, and he listened in great surprise when Nobbly told him all about what he had seen the night before.

"Yes, I tell you," said Nobbly, all excited. "That nasty, unkind gnome came into my room in the middle of the night, hid himself at the end of my bed, and then when I woke up, I saw his big hands sticking up ready to come at me! Think of that, now! Don't you think you ought to go and take Big-Hands to prison?"

"Well, no, I don't," said Mr Stick. "You see, you might have made a mistake, Nobbly. After all, you didn't see Big-Hands' face, did you? It might have been someone else."

"Fiddlesticks!" said Nobbly, scornfully. "It *couldn't* have been anyone else! No one else has such enormous hands as Big-Hands. I *know* they must have been his hands."

"Well, wait and see if he comes again," said Mr Stick. "I'll wait outside tonight, and if you give me a call I'll come in and take Mr Big-Hands off to prison, if it really *is* him."

"But suppose he escapes before you come?" said Nobbly. "How shall I get hold of him? He is such a big fellow."

"Well," said Mr Stick, thinking hard, "you might take a piece of rope and make a loop in it, Nobbly. Then, if Big-Hands does come again and scares you by sticking up his great hands at the end of the bed, you just throw the loop of rope round them, draw it tight – and you'll have got him prisoner all ready for me to march off!"

"Ooh, that's a *good* idea!" said Nobbly, very pleased. He went home and got a piece of rope. He carefully made a loop in it and put it beside his bed, ready for the night. When his bedtime came he undressed, got into bed, and put the loop of rope under his pillow. Aha, Mr Big-Hands, just wait!

He fell asleep – and woke again with a jump just after midnight. And dear me, bless us all, there were his great, bony feet sticking up again in the moonlight, looking like enormous hands!

"Oh, it's you, Big-Hands, again, is it!" cried Nobbly, and he fished under the pillow for his loop of rope. In a trice he had it out and threw it neatly over what he thought were the hands at the foot of the bed – but of course they were his own feet! He pulled the loop tight, and then gave a scream!

"Oh, oh, let go my feet, Big-Hands! Oh, you wicked goblin, you've got my feet!

"Ow! Ow! Help! Help!" yelled the gnome, and rolled off the bed with a bump. He tried to get up, but of course his feet were tied together, and he fell over each time he tried. He was really dreadfully frightened.

"Mr Stick, Mr Stick, come and help me!" he called. "Big-Hands has got me by the feet and won't let go!"

Now Mr Stick had been hiding in the garden, as he promised – but he had fallen asleep. He woke up in a hurry when he heard such a yelling and shouting going on. He jumped up – and at the same moment Big-Hands the goblin, who had been fast asleep next door, and had been awakened by the dreadful yells and shouts from Nobbly, rushed out of his cottage.

"What's the matter, what's the matter?" called Big-Hands, running up the path and bumping into Mr Stick, the

policeman, who was most
surprised to see Big-Hands, for
he thought he must be hiding
upstairs inside Nobbly's cottage,
frightening him!

The two of them opened the
door and rushed up the stairs,
Nobbly was still shouting and
yelling, rolling about on the floor
with his feet tied tightly together
by the loop of rope.

"Come on, quick, someone's
hurting poor Nobbly!" cried Big-
Hands, all his quarrel with the
gnome quite forgotten. Up the
stairs they rushed, both of them,
and flung open the bedroom
door. It was quite dark in the

bedroom, and Mr Stick shone his lantern round.

Nobbly was panting on the floor, pulling with all his might at his rope! Mr Stick set his lantern down on a table and lifted Nobbly to his feet.

"Someone's tied your feet together," said Big-Hands, in astonishment, as he saw the loop of rope tied tightly round the gnome's bony feet. "Whoever did that?"

"Why, wasn't it *you*?" said Nobbly in amazement, staring at Big-Hands.

"No, indeed it wasn't," answered Big-Hands at once. "I

wouldn't do such a horrid thing! You ought to know that. Besides, Mr Stick the policemen will tell you I came rushing up the stairs with him – I wasn't in your bedroom at all. I do wonder who it was. Let's hunt round a bit and see if we can see a robber, shall we, Mr Stick?"

They untied poor Nobbly's feet and then, taking the lantern, they all hunted round the cottage – but, of course there was no one there at all! They couldn't understand it.

"I'm so frightened!" wept Nobbly. "I can't make it out. Who is this person with great, enormous hands who keeps coming to frighten me? Oh, dear Big-Hands, do please stay with me for the rest of the night and sleep here so that I shan't be alone. Then, if the person comes again, you will be able to scare him away for me. You are so very brave."

"Very well," promised Big-Hands. So they said goodnight to Mr Stick, and off he went home. Big-Hands and Nobbly settled down to sleep in the bed – it was rather a tight fit for two people – and soon nothing was to be heard but gentle snores from Nobbly and enormously loud ones from Big-Hands.

Well, Big-Hands suddenly gave such a tremendous snore that Nobbly woke up with a jump – and goodness me, there were his feet again, sticking up in the moonlight just like big hands coming to get him.

"Ooh! Ow!" yelled Nobbly, in a fright. "Wake up, Big-Hands! Look! Look!"

Big-Hands woke up with a jump and sat up in the moonlight. He saw at once what Nobbly was looking at – but he was wiser than the foolish gnome, and he knew that what Nobbly thought were hands,

were really his own bony feet
with the bed-clothes off! He
began to laugh. How Big-Hands
laughed!

He rolled over and over in the
bed, dragging all the clothes
from Nobbly and making him
shiver with cold.

"Ho ho ho, ha ha ha, hee hee
hee!" yelled Big-Hands, the tears
pouring down his cheeks. "Oh,
Nobbly you'll be the death of
me, really you will! It's your own
silly big feet looking at you, not
a robber's hands at all! Oh my,
oh my, I've got such a terrible
stitch in my side! Whatever will
you do next?"

Well, when Nobbly looked a little closer, and waggled his toes about to see if the hands really were his feet, he found that Big-Hands was right – and he went as red as a cooked beetroot! You should have seen him. He did feel so ashamed of himself. Whatever would Mr Stick say? And what would all the people of the village say too, when they heard the funny tale of how Nobbly had been scared of his own feet – and had even tied them up in a loop of rope, and rolled about the floor! Oh dear! What a dreadful silly he was, to be sure.

"Oh, Nobbly, you'll be the joke of the town tomorrow!" laughed Big-Hands, wiping the tears of laughter from his eyes.

"Big-Hands, don't tell anyone," said Nobbly, in a small voice. "Please be friends with me again – and don't tell anybody about this. I do hate to be laughed at."

"Well, you deserve to be," said Big-Hands. "You have been very unkind lately, Nobbly – chasing my cat, and throwing rubbish into my garden, and letting your bonfire smoke come into my kitchen, and playing your music when I am trying to have a nap. You don't deserve any kindness from me. No – I think everyone must hear this funny story about you. It's *such* a joke!"

"Oh please, Big-Hands, I know I've been unkind and horrid," wept the gnome. "But I won't be again. I do want to be friends with you. You were so kind to stay with me tonight. I will buy your cat a nice fresh fish from the fishmonger each day for a fortnight if you will forgive me, and promise not to tell anyone about it at all."

"Well, that's a kind thought of yours," said Big-Hands, who was always pleased when anyone was good to his cat. "I'll forgive you and be friends again, then, Nobbly. But you won't mind if I have a good laugh now and again, will you, when I think about tonight? For really it was very, very funny!"

So now the two are great friends once more, and Big-Hands' cat couldn't understand her good luck when she was given a fish each day by Nobbly the gnome!

And, sometimes, when Nobbly is a bit silly and does foolish things, Big-Hands looks at him with a twinkle in his eye, and begins to laugh.

"Do you remember when you

caught your own feet instead of a robber?" he chuckles. Then Nobbly goes red, and stops being silly. He does so hate to be reminded of the night when he thought his feet were hands!

The Lucky
Jackdaw

ONCE upon a time there was a little girl called Fiona, who found a baby jackdaw on the ground. He had fallen from a nest in the church tower, and couldn't fly back.

"You poor little thing!" said Fiona. I'll take you home and look after you till you're well enough to fly away."

So she took him home and found a cardboard box which she stuffed with straw. She put the little black creature into it and then went to find some bread and milk.

"Good gracious!" said her aunt. "Whatever will you bring

into the house next? You
brought a stray cat last month
that stole the joint out of the
larder. Last week you found a
stray dog with a bad leg, and it
chased our chickens as soon as it
got better. Now you've got a
wretched little jackdaw who will
steal everything shiny and bright
he can lay his beak on, as soon as
he can fly!"

"Oh please, Auntie, let me
look after him," begged Fiona,
who was so kind-hearted that she
really couldn't leave any small or
hurt creature by itself. "I'll keep
him in the shed outside if only
you'll let me look after him. I'm

sure he'll fly away as soon as he's big enough."

"Very well," grumbled her aunt. "I suppose you can keep it if you like. But if that bird steals any thimbles of mine, I'll punish you, so there!"

So Fiona kept the jackdaw in the shed outside. She had to feed it many times a day, for it was a hungry little thing. She put bread soaked with milk on the end of a pointed stick, and the little creature took it greedily. It grew very quickly, and soon had a fine pair of strong, black wings. But it didn't fly away! It was so fond of Fiona that wherever she went it

went too, and even if she went
for a walk, the jackdaw flew
along with her, circling round her
head and calling, "Chack! Chack!
Chack! Chack!"

Then he began to be naughty.
He went into the house one day
and saw Fiona's aunt sewing. She
put her bright thimble down for
a moment, and Jack caught it up
in his beak. In a trice he was out
of the window, and had hidden
the thimble in a hole right up in
the thatch.

"Oh, you wicked bird!" cried
Fiona's aunt. "Bring me that
thimble back at once! Fiona!
Fiona! Where are you? That

jackdaw of yours has taken my
thimble! I told you that was what
would happen!"

Fiona called Jack and made
him bring back the silver
thimble. Then she scolded him
hard, and he sat on the fence and
hung his head.

But it didn't make him mend his ways. Whenever he saw anything bright and gleaming he picked it up in his beak and flew off with it. Fiona's aunt was angry, and she said she wouldn't have Jack in her shed if he didn't stop his wicked ways.

Fiona was very miserable. She was fond of Jack, and couldn't bear to think that he might have to leave. Her aunt scolded her all day long, not because she was a nasty lady, but just because she was very worried about a lot of things.

"Your uncle hasn't been able to work for a month because of his bad leg," she said. "And the hens are not laying and the cows are not giving enough milk. Where is the money going to come from to pay the rent? I really don't know. The shoemaker wants his bill paid, too. You'll have to help me a little more, Fiona, to make up for that horrid bird of yours always worrying me. I'm sure he took the money I put on the dresser yesterday."

Poor Fiona! She worked hard from morning to night to help her aunt. She fed the hens and milked the cows, she looked after her uncle and did everything she possibly could.

She begged her aunt not to get rid of her Jackdaw, but she wouldn't promise.

"If only the bird would pay you back for your kindness to it!" she said. "If it was a hen it could lay eggs! But it just does nothing but steal things."

Now the jackdaw knew that the aunt hated him, and he was very unhappy. He flew off by himself one day, and came to a buttercup field. He fluttered down to the river that flowed through it, and as he walked down to the water to have a drink something very bright caught his eye.

It was a ring. It lay in the water

near the bank, and seemed to wink at him as the stream went rushing over it. Jack thought it was very pretty indeed. He put his head into the water and pulled out the ring.

It shone even more brightly. It had three great big shiny stones in it, and Jack pecked at them. But they were held tightly in the ring, and he could not get them out. So he decided to take the ring back home with him and show it to Fiona.

Off he went. Fiona was sitting peeling potatoes with her aunt, and they were talking together.

"Mr Brown told me this

morning that Lady Penelope went out in a boat on the river yesterday and lost her beautiful diamond ring," said Fiona's aunt. "I expect that it will never be seen again! They say it is worth a lot of money!"

"Is it worth as much as a hundred pounds?" asked Fiona.

"Oh, the ring will be worth much, much more than that!" said her aunt. "Why, there's a reward of a hundred pounds offered to anyone who manages to find it."

When Jack heard this he gave such a squawk that Fiona's aunt jumped and dropped her potato knife on the floor.

"There's that horrid bird again!" she said. "I'll have someone take him away tomorrow, I really will!"

Jack squawked again and hopped up to her. He dropped the ring right into her lap and then stood with his head cocked on one side to see what she would do with it.

The woman picked up the diamond ring and looked at it in the greatest astonishment. For a moment she could hardly speak. The she found her tongue. "Fiona!" she said. "Fiona! I do believe this is the ring that Lady

Penelope lost! Your jackdaw
must have found it in the river!"

"Oh, Auntie!" cried Fiona in
delight. "Then we shall get the
hundred pounds! And you can
pay the rent and the shoemaker
and the doctor, and will have
plenty of money left over!"

"Put on your hat and come
with me to the house where Lady
Penelope lives," said her aunt, in
great excitement. So Fiona got
her hat and then she and her
aunt set out for the big house
which belonged to Lady
Penelope. Jack went along too,
flying round their heads and
shouting, "Chack! Chack!" as

loudly as he could. And for once
Fiona's aunt didn't scold him.

At last they arrived at the
house. The butler took them into
a big room, and Lady Penelope
came in to see them. As soon as
she saw the ring she cried out
with joy, and took it from
Fiona's aunt.

"Wherever *did* you find it!" she
cried. "What part of the river
was it in?"

"Our jackdaw found it," said
Fiona.

"Chack! Chack!" cried the
jackdaw outside the window.
Lady Penelope thought he really
was the cleverest bird she had

ever seen.

"I found him when he was a baby," said Fiona. "I looked after him till he was big, but he wouldn't fly away. He stayed with me all the time. Sometimes he is very naughty, but now he really has been very good we shall have to make a fuss of him! You won't want to get rid of him now, will you, Auntie?"

"No," said her aunt. "He really has paid you back for your kindness to him, Fiona!"

"And I must pay you your reward!" said Lady Penelope. "I will send the money this evening when I have managed to get it from the bank."

Off went Fiona and her aunt again, very, very happy, for all their troubles were gone. The jackdaw knew they were glad and he shouted loudly all the way home.

The money came that day. Fiona's aunt paid all her bills, bought some more hens, and a pretty new frock for herself. Fiona had a new hat and two new dresses, and a pair of pretty blue shoes.

They wanted to give Jack a present, too, but all they could think of was a little bit of nice fresh meat, which he ate greedily.

Fiona's aunt never said another word against him. In fact, she became very fond of him, and after that she always let Fiona look after any stray animal or bird that she found, so the little girl was very happy.

As for Jack, he lives with them still – but if you go to see Fiona, be careful not to leave your money about! He is still very naughty at times!

A Story of Tidiness and Untidiness

THERE were once two little girls called Hilda and Joan. They were twins and did everything together.

One day their little brother got measles, and Mother was dreadfully afraid Hilda and Joan would get it too.

"I wonder who would have you to stay with him for a little while?" she said. "You can't go to Aunt Kate's, she's away. I wonder if Great Aunt Jane would have you!"

Mother wrote to see. Great Aunt Jane said yes, she would have Hilda and Joan, but they would have to make themselves useful around the house.

"Well, you two girls know how to dust and sweep and make your own beds," said Mother, "so you must just offer to do that for Great Aunt Jane."

Off went Hilda and Joan, rather excited to be going away to stay, and quite determined to do all they could to help their great aunt.

Great Aunt Jane lived in a dear little cottage, with a lovely garden full of flowers. She had two little puppies and a tiny kitten that played with them all day long. In the garden she had a little round pond with goldfish in it. Hilda and Joan were very excited when they saw all these lovely things.

"Puppies and a kitten to play with!" said Hilda.

"And a goldfish pond to sail boats on!" cried Joan. "What fun we'll have."

The next morning Great Aunt called them into her kitchen, where she was busy feeding the puppies and the kitten.

"I told Mother you would have to make yourselves useful around the house," she said, looking at them over the top of her big spectacles. "What can you be trusted to do? Girls don't work half as well nowadays as they used to in *my* young days."

"Great Aunt, we *will* work well!" said Joan. "We can be trusted to do lots of things. We can dust and sweep and make our beds."

"Very well. Make your beds each morning. And Hilda, you can dust the dining-room and sweep it and Joan can dust and sweep the drawing-room. Keep your own room tidy too. I'll come and watch you this morning. You'll have to work hard, you see."

Great Aunt Jane chuckled at the twins.

They laughed.

"Oh, that isn't much!" said Hilda. "We shall soon get that done! Then we'll be able to play in the garden with the puppies, won't we?"

"Yes, you may," said Great Aunt. "But you MUST do your jobs thoroughly, do you understand? A job which is only half done is a disgrace to any girl or boy!"

Then she took them upstairs and watched them while they made their beds and tidied their room. Then downstairs they went and showed her how they dusted and swept.

"That's very nice, very nice indeed," said Great Aunt Jane. "I hope you'll do it like that every morning."

The twins ran out into the garden.

"Isn't Great Aunt particular?" said Hilda. "It's an awful bother to dust in every corner like that."

"Well, Mother's particular too," said Joan, who liked doing things well.

Hilda didn't. She was an untidy little girl, and she usually left everything for Joan to do. But she couldn't at Great Aunt's because they each had different things to do.

119

The next day both little girls did their morning jobs. They turned their mattresses, plumped up the pillows, and made their beds beautifully. And each of them dusted and swept as carefully as could be. Then out they went to play with the puppies and to watch the goldfish as it swam.

But the *next* morning, Hilda couldn't be bothered to dust properly.

"What does it matter if I leave the dark corners undusted!" she thought. "Nobody will see if I don't do them! And I *do* so want to go out into the garden and see what it can be that those puppies are squealing about!"

So out she went long before Joan, who was giving the drawing-room a very good dusting.

Next morning it was just the same. Hilda didn't bother a bit about dusting in the corners. Nor did she on the next day, which was Saturday. She was out in the garden long before Joan.

But as Joan was dusting carefully behind a big saucer on the china cabinet, she came across a funny little flat parcel.

She picked it up. On it was written, "For Joan, with Great

Aunt's love. Buy a ship with this to sail on the goldfish pond."

Joan opened it. Inside was some money!

"Oh, how lovely!" cried Joan, rushing to thank Great Aunt Jane. "What a good thing it was that I remembered to dust behind that saucer!"

She ran to show Hilda. Hilda was delighted to think they would have a ship to sail on the pond, but a little bit hurt because Aunt Jane hadn't given her some money, too. They bought a lovely ship and had a glorious time sailing it on the pond. Hilda did so wish she had one as well.

The days went by and the little girls did their work every morning. Great Aunt Jane never seemed to go and look how they were doing it, so Hilda started to become more and more careless. She made her bed badly, and she didn't turn the mattress once. The next Saturday that came she bundled her bed together anyhow, and ran quickly downstairs to sail the boat before Joan came.

But Joan was a long time coming! She had made a lovely discovery. As she made her bed she saw something long and flat lying beneath the mattress. She picked it up and undid the paper. It was a book of fairy-tales, with lots and lots of pictures!

"How perfectly lovely!" cried Joan, and ran to thank Great Aunt Jane again.

"I'm glad you like it," said Great Aunt, smiling at her. "I know you must have made your bed properly, my dear, if you found that."

When Joan showed the book to Hilda, Hilda began to cry.

"Nasty old Aunt Jane, to give you things and not me!" she sobbed. "Mother always gives us the same. Why doesn't Great Aunt Jane?"

Just at that moment Great Aunt came out.

"Dear, dear, dear!" she said. "What's all this to-do?"

"Hilda's crying because you didn't give anything to her," said Joan. "Why didn't you, Great Aunt?"

"Oh, but I *did*!" said Great Aunt. "Come and see."

She took the two little girls into the dining-room which Hilda was supposed to dust each morning.

"Did you dust behind the clock on the mantelpiece?" she asked Hilda.

Hilda went very red. She knew there were lots of corners in the room she had missed.

"No," she said, "I didn't."

"There now!" said Aunt Jane. "And I put some money for you there last Saturday, because I wanted to pay you for dusting so nicely. Well, well. I must have it back, as you didn't dust properly. See if it's there."

Hilda peeped behind the clock. Yes, there was a little flat parcel with "Hilda" written on it. And wasn't it dusty!

Great Aunt solemnly undid the parcel and put the money back into her purse.

Then she took them upstairs to their bedroom.

"Did you turn your mattress this morning?" she asked Hilda.

Hilda hung her head and said no, she hadn't.

"Dear, dear, dear!" said Aunt Jane. "Then I suppose your fairy-tale book is still under the mattress! Why don't you take a look and see!"

It was! And very sadly Hilda watched Great Aunt put it away in a cupboard. She was terribly ashamed and made up her mind never ever to do her work carelessly again.

"You are going home today," said Great Aunt Jane, "and you may each take a puppy for your own, because I have enjoyed having you. Joan, go on doing your jobs well, and some day you will make a fine little wife. Hilda, don't forget the lesson you have learnt while you have been here with me!"

And the funny old lady smiled at them so kindly, that Hilda smiled back through her tears and thought what a silly girl she had been.

Then the twins went upstairs, packed up all their things in their bags, tucked their puppies under their arms, and went downstairs again to say goodbye to Great Aunt Jane.

When Hilda said goodbye to her great aunt, she kissed her and whispered something into her ear.

"I'm sorry I worked so very badly," she said, "but I promise I never will again."

Great Aunt waved goodbye to them as they went off. The twins were sorry to leave the dear little cottage, but they were most excited to be going home to Mother and Daddy again.

"Whatever do you think Mother will say when she sees our puppies?" said Joan.

Mother was delighted to have her two little girls home again, and she loved the puppies. She wondered why Joan had a ship and a book as well, while Hilda had none, but she asked no questions.

But she *was* surprised to find, after only a few days, that instead of one very tidy little girl and one very *untidy* little girl, she had two of the tidiest little daughters you can imagine.

She couldn't make it out. Hilda's bed was always as well made as Joan's, and instead of hurry-scurrying over it, and getting everything done first, she found that Hilda was often longer than Joan.

"Well, really!" said Mother to Daddy one night. "I honestly don't believe any mother has got two such thorough little girls as we have, Daddy. I really don't think you'd be able to find a single speck of dust anywhere in the house, no matter how hard you looked!"

Hilda and Joan were very pleased to hear that, and Hilda was delighted when Mother took up her pen the next morning, and said she really must write and tell Great Aunt Jane how helpful the twins were.

The letter was written and sent. Two days afterwards there came

a great rat-tat-tat at the door.
Mother opened it, and took a
big, exciting-looking parcel from
the postman.

"Why, it's addressed to Hilda!"
she said.

Hilda was most excited. She
undid the string and opened the
parcel.

Inside was a lovely fairy-tale
book! There was a letter too, and
when Hilda opened it, some
money fell out!

"Dear Hilda," wrote Great
Aunt, "I think these belong to
you now, don't they? If you buy a
ship like Joan's, do please come
and stay with me again and sail it

on my pond. Don't forget to come soon, will you?"

Wasn't that nice of Great Aunt Jane?

When Mollie Missed the Bus

MOLLIE had gone to tea with Peter. It was a lovely, sunny afternoon, so the two children had their tea together in the garden. Peter's mother brought out a lovely feast for them – buttered scones with honey, jam sponge and ginger biscuits.

"Oh, Mother – what a delicious tea you made for us!" said Peter. "I wish I could do something for you in return!"

"You can," said Mother, laughing at him. "You and Mollie can take butterfly nets after tea and go and catch those tiresome white butterflies that are laying eggs on Daddy's cabbages. The caterpillars will eat up all the leaves if we don't do something about it."

"Right," said Peter. "We'll do that for you."

So after tea the two children got butterfly nets and went to catch the tiresome butterflies. But they didn't see any butterflies at all at first, so they picked scores of green caterpillars out of the cabbages, instead.

"They've eaten nearly the whole of this cabbage heart away!" said Mollie. "Oh, look, Peter, – *there's* a butterfly!"

Then others came and soon the children were trying to catch them all in their nets. Suddenly Peter called out:

"I say – look! Here's an *enormous* one! It's coming your way, Mollie. Catch it!"

It certainly was an enormous one. But when it saw Mollie's net it flew back towards Peter again. Crash! He brought his net straight down on it.

"Got it!" he cried. "Come and see, Mollie."

They both peered through the netting in which the butterfly was caught firmly. Mollie gave a startled cry.

"It isn't a butterfly! It's – it's – Oh, Peter, it can't be a real, live pixie, can it?"

"Of course not," said Peter. "Fairies aren't real. I don't believe in them. Don't be such a silly, Mollie."

"But look, Peter – it's got a little face – and golden hair – and hands and feet," said Mollie, in excitement. "Goodness – we have caught a fairy! And I've never, ever seen a fairy in my whole life before!"

Peter raised the net carefully and clapped down his hand on the tiny creature inside. There was a squeal.

"Peter, don't do that, don't! You're hurting the poor little thing," said Mollie. "Put it down. It *is* a fairy!"

"Of course I'm a fairy," said a tiny, high voice. "I'm Pippy the pixie. Let me go, you're hurting. How dare you catch me in your net?"

"You're not a pixie," said Peter, still holding tight. "There are no such things. You're really some strange kind of butterfly, aren't you?"

"You're *hurting* me! You're squashing my wings. Let me go, I said," cried the pixie, squealing out again.

"Certainly not," said Peter.
"I'm going to put you into a box
with some holes in and send you
up to a museum to find your
right name, and..."

"No, no, no!" cried the pixie
and tears fell down on to Peter's
hand. "I'll die if you put me in a
matchbox!" She turned to
Mollie. "Please make him let me
go!" she begged her. "I can
hardly breathe, he's squashing
me so."

"Peter – let her go," said
Mollie. "You're unkind and very
silly. Even if you *don't* believe in
fairies, surely you can see one
when she's under your nose. If

you don't let her go, I'll go and tell your mother – *she'll* know a fairy when she sees one!"

"I shan't let her go," said Peter, obstinately, and squeezed the pixie still more tightly. She screamed, and her head drooped forward.

"You're killing her!" cried Mollie, and she gave Peter a good wallop on the back. He was so surprised to think of the gentle Mollie hitting him so hard that he opened his hand – and out flew the pixie!

"Thank you, kind girl!" she called to Mollie. "Thank you! I'll return your kindness as soon as I possibly can."

Peter sulked. He didn't know what to say or think. Mollie tried to make up to him for hitting him. She felt very ashamed of that now.

"Let's go down to your lily pond and sail all your boats," she said at last. Peter cheered up a bit at that. He went to fetch an armful of small boats, and soon they were bobbing merrily over the water.

"Mollie! Don't forget your bus!" called a voice from the house suddenly. "It will soon be at the corner."

"Oh dear," said Mollie,

scrambling up, "I didn't know it was nearly time. I must go, Peter. Mother said if I missed the bus she wouldn't let me stay up to supper tonight – and Granny's coming this afternoon, so I really *must*!"

She got her hat and then ran to the front gate. Peter came with her. Alas, and alas! There was the bus sailing merrily round the corner, full of passengers! Mollie had missed it.

She went back into the garden, crying. "Now Mother will be *really* cross," she said.

A tiny voice called to her, "What's the matter?"

Mollie looked up. Pippy the pixie was sitting there right beside her, swinging up and down on a honeysuckle twig.

"I wanted to catch that bus," she said. "And I missed it. Oh dear – my mother will be so cross with me for not catching it."

"I'll catch it for you," said the pixie. "Where is it?"

"It's gone round the corner. Anyway, you couldn't possibly catch it – and even if you did it wouldn't come back here for me," said Mollie.

The pixie flew down to the ground and picked up Peter's butterfly net, which was still there. It was very heavy for her to carry, but she managed it.

"I'm off to catch the bus for you," she said, and flew right over the house!

"Whatever does she mean?" said Mollie, staring. "Peter, do you still not believe in fairies?"

"I'll believe in them if that pixie brings the bus back for you," said Peter, grinning. "But I know she won't. I wonder what she can be thinking of doing with my net?"

Pippy was doing something strange. She flew to the corner of the road and saw the bus far away in the distance. She flew

after it, still carrying the net.
When she got near to it, she
chanted a strange little spell. At
once the handle of the net
became longer and longer and
longer, and the net part grew
wider and wider wider and very,
very *big*.

It reached the bus. It hovered
over it! The passengers on the
top looked at it and screamed.
They began to hurry quickly
down the stairs of the bus, calling
out in alarm.

The passengers down below
were frightened and jumped off,
too. The driver and conductor
leapt down. What was this

strange, horrid white thing that
was held right over their big bus?

Then whoooooosh! Down
came the net and caught the bus!
Everyone fled at once.

The net then grew smaller. So
did the bus inside. The net
turned itself upside down, and
held the bus neatly there, both
net and bus getting smaller as the
handle of the net gradually got
shorter and shorter.

At last the pixie could handle it
again properly. She flew back to
Mollie and Peter with it, looking
very pleased.

"I've caught the bus for you,"
she said, and neatly tipped it out

on the grass. "There you are – It's nice, isn't it? – Though I really can't think *why* you want to catch these buses."

Mollie and Peter stared in astonishment and alarm at the tiny bus. What in the world had happened? It was *exactly* like the real buses that went up and down the road, but it was very, very small.

"Mollie!" called Peter's mother's voice. "Did you miss the bus? Silly child! Come here, quickly, because Peter's father has got the car, and he'll run you home."

Mollie didn't dare to disobey.

Clutching the tiny bus in her hand she ran to the front gates where Peter's father was waiting with his car.

"Jump in quickly," he said. "I've not got much time." Off they went. Mollie hadn't a word to say. She was feeling so very, very puzzled. As they went down the road, they came to a crowd of people, talking excitedly together. Peter's father drew up in the car.

"What is it?" he called, and then everyone started talking to him at once.

"It's our bus! It's vanished!"

"A great big thing like a giant

net came over it, and we all got out in a hurry, I can tell you!"

"The net caught the bus – and then it seemed to disappear – got so small that we couldn't see where it went."

"Anyway, it's gone, and hasn't come back – and here we all are, stranded – waiting for the next bus to come along!"

Mollie listened in amazement. Oh dear, oh dear, it was all because of her that this had happened. That silly little pixie must have thought buses were caught in nets, in exactly the same way that butterflies were. She had gone to catch the bus for

Mollie, she had made it shrink –
and, at this very moment the
little girl was holding the bus in
her hand!

She managed to slip out of the
car while Peter's father was
talking to everyone and no one
saw her when she popped the
tiny bus down in the gutter and
left it there.

"Perhaps if it grows big again
everything will be alright," she
thought. "I'll just take one of the
little seat-cushions with me, then
I'll know for certain if the bus
has grown big, because someone
will be surprised when they find
out there is a seat-cushion

missing and so I shall be sure to hear all about it."

She went off home in the car, very silent. Peter's father was puzzled and rather scornful of everything the people had told him about the bus.

"All this nonsense about a giant net catching the bus and taking it away!" he said. "Whatever next?"

But the next day he was even more astonished to hear that the bus had been found again – in the very same place where everyone said it had been caught by the giant net. It was its own size again, of course.

"But there's a seat-cushion missing," said the conductor to everyone. "Fancy that! It's too peculiar for words, isn't it?"

It was. Nobody could understand such a mysterious happening. Mollie told her mother all about it, but alas, she didn't believe a world of it!

"Silly girl!" she said to Mollie. "Making up such a stupid fairy-tale! You're too old to believe in fairies. Peter doesn't, you know."

But Peter does! How could he help it when that pixie brought back the bus in his butterfly net? And, of course, Mollie still has the tiny little seat-cushion. She's got it in her own toy bus, and it's her most precious possession.

She showed it to me one afternoon and told me the whole story. That's why I was able to tell it to you, of course!

The Lost Ring

JEAN was a little girl with curly hair and blue eyes. She would have been a dear little girl if only she hadn't been so proud of herself.

"I'm so very glad I'm pretty!" she used to say as she looked in the mirror.

"I'm glad I've got curly hair! I wish I had some beads to wear round my neck, and rings to wear on my fingers."

When Jean's birthday came, she liked her Granny's present best of all.

"Oh, look!" she cried. "It's a lovely little gold ring with a pretty blue stone!

Oh, how wonderful! I've always wanted one to wear!"

"It's too big for you to wear now" said Granny. "You must keep it till you are eighteen. Take great care of it, Jean."

Jean slipped the ring on to her biggest finger. It certainly was too big, but how pretty it was!

"Thank you, Granny!" she said. "I do wish I could wear it."

And then one day she did! It happened like this. Uncle Robin was having a party, and he asked Jean if she would go. Of course she was delighted, and Mummy bought her a new frock to go in. It was blue, and she had a blue ribbon in her hair.

"Oh dear! I wish I could wear my little ring with the blue stone!" she thought. "Then I'd be all blue!" She ran upstairs, and looked at the ring.

Then the naughty little girl suddenly slipped the ring on her finger, closed the jewel-case, and ran downstairs again.

She arrived at the party in good time. and was soon playing games with the others. She showed all the other children her ring, and they thought it was lovely. Jean was very proud.

After tea her uncle said, "Now then! Who's coming for a row on the lake with me!"

Of course everyone wanted to go, and off they all sped.

"Three at a time!" said Uncle Robin, stepping into the boat. Jean and two other little girls got into the boat and sat down. Uncle Robin began to row, and off the boat glided over the water.

"The water does feel so nice and cool," said one little girl, dabbling her hand in the lake.

Jean put hers in too. It did feel lovely and cool, and she liked it.

But oh dear me! She had forgotten all about her ring! It was so loose that it easily slipped off her finger and went down, down, down through the water.

When Jean remembered her ring, she quickly pulled her hand in and looked at it. But the ring was gone!

"Oh! oh!" she cried, with tears running down her cheeks. "Uncle Robin! Uncle Robin! My ring has fallen into the lake!"

Of course, Uncle Robin was very sorry, but of course nothing could be done. The ring was quite lost.

Poor Jean cried and cried. She didn't know what Mummy and Granny would say when they heard she had been disobedient and worn her ring – and lost it!

When Mummy heard what had happened she was very sorry, but she didn't scold Jean much, because she saw how unhappy she was.

But Granny scolded her hard.

"You're a vain, conceited little girl," she said, "and you're not to be trusted with nice things."

"I'm very sorry, Granny," said poor Jean. "I promise I won't be vain any more. Please give me another chance."

Of course Granny gave her another chance, and forgave her. And Jean really did keep her word and was as good as gold after that.

But that's not the end of the story. For one day Uncle Robin went fishing in the lake and caught a fine big fish.

He sent it to Jean's Granny with his love. And when Granny got it ready for cooking, what do you think she found inside it?

The little gold ring! Wasn't that

an extraordinary thing?

And what do you think Granny did? She took it straight to Jean and gave it to her once more.

"Here is you ring again, Jean," she said. "A fish swallowed it, and it was found inside. You are not a silly, vain little girl any more, so I am giving you your ring to keep again!"

And you can just imagine how delighted Jean was.

The
Wind s Party

"I want to blow hard!" said the autumn wind. "I want to rush round and sweep things away in front of me. I haven't had a good blow for ages."

"Well, blow then," said a little cloud. "I think I shall rather like it if you do!"

"I don't want to waste all my breath on a little thing like *you*!" said the wind. "I want to blow hundreds and thousands of things away. I want to have some real fun."

"Well, have a party, and ask the trees to come to it!" said the little cloud. "Tell them to put on party dresses of all colours – and

then blow as hard as you can!
You'll have such fun blowing off
their red, yellow, orange and
brown leaves!"

"That's a good idea!" said the
wind. "I could blow the leaves
high in the air, and all round
about – and then I could puff
them along the ground, and
sweep them into the ditches. I
think I could really have some
fun doing that."

So the wind went round about
whispering in among all the
trees. "Come to a party, all of
you! Come to a party! Put on
your prettiest colours, and come
to the wind's party!"

The beech put on a dress of brightest gold, and shimmered in the sunshine. The hazel put on pale gold and so did the silver birch.

The chestnut put on orange and yellow, and the wild cherry put on the brightest pink. The oak turned a russet brown, and the creeper on the houses nearby flamed into crimson.

"Fine, fine!" cried the wind, as he swept around. "Are you ready for the party! It's a party for your leaves, you know. I want them to play with, I want to make them dance and twist in the air. Are you ready?"

Then, with a rush, the wind swept through the trees. The frost had touched them the night before, and they were loose. The wind pulled them off.

Then off into the air went the coloured leaves, red, yellow, pink and brown, whirling and twirling, swaying and falling.

What a game the wind had with them! How he blew them about, and made them dance and prance! Soon the trees were bare, for their coloured party frocks were gone!

"Come and play too!" cried the autumn wind to the children. "Come along, come along! For every leaf you catch before it reaches the ground you shall have a happy day next year!"

Let's go and catch them as they whirl in the air. Let's see if we can catch three hundred and sixty-five, a whole year of wonderful, happy days!

We're coming to your party too, autumn wind. Please wait for us, do!

Billy s
Shopping

"BILLY, darling," said Mother one fine morning, "Will you take the shopping basket and go to the shops for me? I want a nice, brown loaf from the baker's, some tea from the grocer's, and a pound of sausages from the butcher's."

"Of course I'll go to the shops for you, Mummy!" said Billy, and he put down his book and jumped up. He took the basket from its place in the corner and went to the door.

"You are a good little boy, Billy," said Mother. "Here is fifty pence for yourself. Buy some sweets or a comic."

"Oh, thank you, Mummy!" said Billy, and off he went. He went to the baker's first where he bought a fine, brown loaf. Then he went to the grocer's and asked for a packet of tea. Lastly, he went to the butcher's and waited in the queue for a pound of sausages. They all went nicely into his basket.

"Now I have my fifty pence to spend," thought Billy. He ran along to the sweet-shop – but on the way he came to the greengrocer's. Oh, what a lovely lot of apples, pears and plums he could see in the window! There they all lay, red, yellow and purple, and Billy stood and looked at them in the greatest delight.

The apples were twenty-five pence each. Billy remembered that his mother loved to eat apples. He could buy her one – a nice, rosy, red one! Then he remembered his little sister Nell. Perhaps he could buy her a plum for twenty-five pence too. That would be a good way to spend his fifty pence. How surprised Mother and Nell would be when he came home and gave them the fruit!

"Yes, that's it," he said to himself, "I will buy a ripe, red

apple for Mother and a juicy
plum for Nell!"

He went into the shop.

"Please may I have an apple
and a plum?" he asked the
shopkeeper. He put his money
down on the counter. The
shopkeeper put a big, rosy apple
and a ripe, purple plum into a
paper bag and gave them to
Billy. He popped them both into
his basket, and galloped home
like a horse!

"I've bought an apple for you,
Mother, and a plum for Nell!" he
said when he had arrived back at
his house. How surprised and
pleased they were!

"I really do think you are the kindest little boy in the world, Billy!" said Mother, and she kissed him.

"Give Billy one of the new chocolate cakes you have made this morning, Mother," said Nell. "He has spent his own money on us, and has bought us some lovely fruit – so we really must give him something too!"

"Oooh! I do love chocolate cakes!" said Billy. Then down they all sat. Mother ate her apple and she said it was very sweet. Nell ate her plum and she said it was very juicy. Billy ate his cake and he said it was by far the nicest chocolate cake he had ever tasted!

So they were all very happy indeed!

Jack and Jill and their Apples

"MOTHER, may we have a
picnic?" asked Jack and
Jill, running into the kitchen,
where their mother was busy
with some cooking.

"Yes, dears," said Mother. "I
will give you a basket of cakes
and apples between you. Then
you can go and have a really
lovely picnic!"

"Oh, thank you, Mother!" said
the two children. They ran to
fetch their basket. Mother filled
it with cakes and apples. Off
went Jack and Jill, carrying it
between them.

"Let's go right to the top of
Mill Hill," said Jill. "Why don't

we take the dog with us? Bill, Bill, Bill! Come along now, come along, Bill!"

Bill the dog ran after them. He could smell the cakes in the basket! "Wuff, wuff!" They did smell good!

Jack and Jill went all the way up the hill to have a picnic. The basket was very heavy. They had a little rest half-way up and then they started off once more. Just as they were getting near the top, Jill turned and spoke crossly to Jack.

"You are not holding the basket properly!" she said. "I am carrying most of it."

"No, you're not!" said Jack.

"Yes, I am!" said Jill.

"You're certainly *not*!" said Jack, and he took hold of the basket more firmly.

"Wuff, wuff!" said Bill. He didn't like to see the children quarrelling.

Jill pulled hard at the basket. Jack pulled back – and as he wasn't paying any attention to where he was going, he caught his foot on a big stone – and down he fell!

The basket went over. The apples rolled out – and oh dear me, as they were on a steep hillside, they rolled all the way

down the hill, bumpity-bumpity-
bumpity-bumpity-bump! Down
they all rolled as fast as fast
could be!

"Oh, no! Look!" cried Jill, in
alarm. "There go our lovely
apples! Quick, Jack, we must
catch them!"

The children ran after the
rolling apples which were still
going bumpity-bumpity-bumpity
down the hill! Bill the dog ran
too. He was a very clever dog.
He caught one of the apples in
his mouth. The rest of the apples
rolled all the way down to the
bottom of the hill and lay still.
Jack and Jill picked them up, and

then, oh dear, what a pity, they
had to walk all the way up the
hill once more!

"Well, it just serves us right for
being so silly as to quarrel," said
Jack. "We've lost one apple –
and now all the others are
bruised. Don't let's ever quarrel
again, Jill."

"No, we won't," said Jill.

When Jack and Jill reached the
top of the hill they sat down.
They peeled their apples and ate
them. They ate their cakes too –
and Bill had one for himself. He
was pleased.

"Wuff, Wuff!" he said. "Cakes
are much better than apples,

Jack and Jill. What a good thing they didn't roll down to the bottom of the hill, too!"